For Sacha and Amin

Text and illustrations copyright © Sarah Arnold 2018

The right of Sarah Arnold to be identified as the author and illustrator
of this work has been asserted by her in accordance with the
Copyright, Designs and Patents Act, 1988 (United Kingdom).

First published in Great Britain and in the USA in 2018 by
Otter-Barry Books, Little Orchard, Burley Gate, Hereford, HR1 3QS
www.otterbarrybooks.com

A catalogue record for this book is available from the British Library.

ISBN 978-1-91095-935-0

Illustrated with watercolour, photography, photoshop

Printed in China

1 3 5 7 9 8 6 4 2

HOW RUDE!

Sarah Arnold

Otter-Barry BOOKS

Pig was driving along one day,
minding his own business,
when he saw Mole by the side of the road
with an enormous box.

"Hop in!" said Pig.
"I'm going your way. I'll give you a lift."

They loaded Mole's box
onto the car.

It was very heavy.

"So, what's in the box?" asked Pig.

"NONE OF YOUR BUSINESS!"

said Mole.

"HOW RUDE!"

said Pig and he slammed on the brakes.

Pig told his friends, Hippo,
Mouse and Girl, about the box.

"HOW RUDE!" they said.

"But what's in the box?"

"I don't know," said Pig.
"Let's find out!"

They looked through the keyhole.

They listened with a glass.

They rocked it.

They rolled it.

Hippo jumped on it.

They hit it with a hammer...

and threw it down some steps.

Hippo tried his X-ray specs.

But the box was
locked tight shut.

So each of the friends dreamed
of what could be in the box.

Mmmm

cheese

yum

cakes

balloons

pop

They were still wondering and dreaming
when Mole came back with his key.

He was delighted when he saw
his box. He ran over to it,

put the key in the keyhole,

unlocked the door...

and...

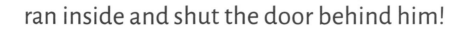
ran inside and shut the door behind him!

"HOW RUDE!"

said the friends.

"He's horrible and mean.
We don't want to speak to him
and we don't care what's in his box!"

NO!

NO!

NO!

NO!

NO!

NO!

NO!

Then the door of the box
opened.

A paw beckoned.
There was a whistle.

Hippo, Girl, Mouse and Pig rushed in.

Mole slammed the door shut!

Ha!

He looked around for some fun,
but there was no one around.

Mole felt lonely.

But then he heard
music...
laughter...
singing...

POP

Yum Yum

Whizz

Mmmm

Oh la la

It was coming from...

the box!

He knocked on the door.
"What are you doing in there?"

POP Yum Yum
Whizz Oh La la
Mmmm

1

"NONE OF YOUR BUSINESS!"

"HOW RUDE!"

said Mole.

But he did so want to
join in the fun.

He picked up his key,
unlocked the door
and...

Whoosh the friends rushed out!

Ha Hee Ha Hee

"Oops WE'RE SORRY!" they said. "We didn't mean to knock you over."

Ha Ha

"I'M SORRY TOO!"
said Mole.
"Please, can we all have fun together?"